AF230285

MICRO-WAVES

A selection

Of micro-fiction

By

John F King

ISBN 978-0-9558519-3-3

York European Publishing 2012

www.johnkingcommunications.co.uk

www.johnkinginternational.eu

Originally from Leeds, **John F King** attended the Universities of

Oxford, York and London.

His interests include cricket and music.

He moved to York while deciding what to do next.

He has lived in York since 1992…

Also available by John F King, York European Publishing:

Wise Guy and other fables

ISBN 978-0-9558519-0-2

Platform Free

ISBN 978-0-9558519-2-6

'The snapshots had become almost as dim as memories.'

Aldous Huxley, Sanary/Mer: **Eyeless in Gaza**

MICRO WAVES

CONTENTS

Endpiece, photo

A QUICK ONE FOR St FRANCIS

Inadvertenly the mint leaf I picked for my tea had a caterpillar on it

Nearly resplendent.

I only realised when I dropped it in the almost boiling water

And started the rescue immediately.

It was as shocked as I was –

What sort of person had I become

What would become of it?

Harmlessly the Daddy Long Legs took up residence in the coil of wires beneath my TV.

I helped it out into the yard

But it took fright and fled, minus the leg it left in my hand.

It was as shocked as I was

I wondered how far it would get

The TV was never the same after that whichever channel I flicked onto.

A WEEK'S A LONG TIME..

I say
What rotten luck
To cop it a week before the show's over
A poet and all, sensitive soul
Couldn't you see it coming?

I know
Maybe he's simply weary
Move him into the sun,
Worked before,
Bring him round?

Depends
On your point of view
Almost feel like laughing
All they've been through
To cop it a week before the show's over

Mind you,
Could almost laugh at the whole jape
Not the weeks the years
All over that mud
Can't tell one uniform from the other

But
Can't tell a soul
Poets, artists living in a hole
Could almost laugh
Almost

By
The way the sun didn't work
This time.

Oxford, Spring 2007,

on seeing Wilfred Owen manuscript in Bodleian library.

AS IF, RIFF 2

If only I could play guitar like Mick Taylor

I owned the rights to Layla

I could write like Frayn

And rain only fell at night

Everything would be alright…

I'd married a Monégasque princess

 In a uniform chocka with self awarded medals and candelabra'd epaules

What a blast!

No past , at least none to think of;

The real impossibility of regret, mess or fright

Everywhere order more pristine than the strictest sect

Sun all day, sea so blue

Politicians of the most benevolent hue

If only all this were true

Nothing to do but swim in you

If only I could control the tide

Set it not too far out or too far in

The sea perfectly stocked with just the right kind of fish

Some exotic to swim with, some to eat

If only God could have kept this prelapsarian feat.

BLUES DUES

You wrote major, I said minor.

You might as well face it: you wouldn't have had the hit without me.

I don't want it to go to the lawyers, man,

We were never about that.

It just makes me feel so flat.

All this conflict, discord sowed when there was such sweet harmony.

I said sort it and get back to me, don't need those 'see you in court' blues.

 I'm not asking for everything, not even a half. Twist and shout, in at 10%. Fair dues.

I acknowledge you wrote the song, the concept, but without that crucial chord change it wouldn't

have had the impact. You know that as well as I do. It's why we stopped making music together,

why you stopped speaking to me though I sat by the phone for 20 years.

So 20 years in the charts, let's call it 9% , respect all those years on the road,

humming the right kind of bars.

20 years at 8.9 % - off the top of my head I'd say you owe me 1.5 million euros,

Yes, you heard me, 1.4 , it wouldn't even trouble your accountants.

I'll drop my bank account details on your answerphone, yeah mine's in the Cayman's too, makes things so much simpler, don't you get me?

We haven't spoken for 20 years, you don't even have to now if you don't want to, as long as you do the right thing.

No, I'd never threaten you, man, you know me, it's just justice.

8 % of the royalties and you can carry on never hearing from me,

That's all I ask , fair play.

'Course we were never a real duo, like Paul and John, Mick and Keith, Elton and Bernie.

Wouldn't even dream of bracketing myself with them.

Listen, call it groovy at 6.9% and I'm out of your bandana.

Let's not get heavy man, it's not in the spirit of what we had.

Only I know which island you live on.

CLOSE OF PLAY

The dreams we had as children.

August, another summer slipping away,

Birds high in the sky,

Wickets chalked on the dustbin.

My dad coming home from English Electric;

An over before tea,

Now dinner.

The past, maybe you just grow out of it.

York 2003 Summer / Autumn

ISBN 18446095 88/96

DOWN IN THE SOUTH OF FRANCE

On the train,

Inside on a sunny day but on the move

Travelling backwards -(couldn't understand the SNCF seat reservation system - it makes me sick)-

Into a profounder France.

Turning inland, you can see your reflection in a window

All the things that have or haven't happened since childhood:

In the van with Mum and Dad navigating Pas de Calais before the tunnel was even a vision

From northern England to northern France, nothing too fancy - you have to draw the line somewhere-

To discovering the far south

The forward facing unsubmerged student with all to play for

All in front of me until the past got me in the end.

Soundtrack in my head became so loud with what ifs and has beens and never were's until even Holst couldn't ipod it out.

Of course if you switch tracks there could be almost as much in front of you as behind-

A kind of reverse hindsight

Deposit the past on the platform like a mass of melted vinyl

Get on the right track

Out of the van and into the TGV.

Nice > Lyon, May2010

FRAGMENT OF
SOMETHING SMALLER

She said it didn't matter but it mattered all the same

The atmosphere changed

I felt it wouldn't revert

This time

I'd read so many books

So heavy with meaning, static with advice

There must be a way they can illuminate me

This time

Of course I'd had relationships before

Was I winner or loser, was it spring or autumn?

This time – it's different

So much experience must rest somewhere

In time

Let it.

There will always be stars in the sky, something bigger than you

Matter? Hope? I'm looking for something smaller..

This time

ISBN 1 86226 663 8

THE TRAIN, A VIEW

From the train window

Yellow fields look peaceful despite their violent name

Greenfields lost if they are built on,

Brownfields regained.

A gasometer held up by nothing

A scarecrow, a straw smile, some kind of lesson?

Now an industrial estate, not light

A suburb without a centre,

An analogy? Of what?

There a warehouse primed to sell me merchandise

I don't know I need.

Pylons, trees, a competition, a view of the world.

York, 2003

GET UP, STAND UP (FOR LUCK)

I was watching the news the other day-

The banker called Diamond

The surgeon called Gore

The spokeswoman, called Waters, for the agency that was supposed to hold the floods back

I wonder what happened to her.

I was reading a screenplay the other day –

The beekeeper returning home from his never ending apiculture

'Hi, honey, I'm home'

To no reply

She's flown – the nest.

I called in the phone shop the other day

Due an upgrade

I asked what handsets were available these days-

I wanted to receive calls from a wider range of people

But was told they'd all sold out and couldn't guarantee any more would be coming in.

I started reading the other day

(the television was making me so depressed)

I started with the back flap to decide if I wanted to move forward

But couldn't flick beyond

The titles:

-How to snare a millionaire by a writer who lived on the wrong side of the Elephant and Castle,

How to avoid redundancy in self employment

How to skim 'How to' books

How to avoid cliché

At the end of the day the house was so crammed with self pity

I had to move out.

As I'd spent the mortgage on therapy the place I moved into

Was smaller than before

So I had to decide what to leave behind.

GOODBYE WAVE

You might have emerged out of the sea but I didn't

You might want to wave goodbye but I don't

So it's getting a bit choppy-

I never VHF'd it'd be plain sailing.

Abandon ship? Go ahead

It's too cold to swim after you

There aren't enough lifeboats to go round

Don't be daft about life

Sink or swim – what a cliché

And it isn't going to be me who says it was love down the drain

Breakers wash away pain

Cliché is death, of life, of love

Whichever comes first

You'll never see two waves crash the same.

IF I KNEW THEN WHAT I KNOW NOW (...)

1 EXTERIOR. PERIMETER EARLY MORNING SOUNDS OF SILENCE, DAWN CHORUS OF BIRDS, SUDDEN DEAFENING ROAR OF AIRCRAFT, THE FOLLOWING EXCHANGE IS PUNCTUATED BY CYCLE OF AIRCRAFT ROAR AND NATURAL SOUNDS OF AN EARLY MORNING)

1   **CHAZ**   Wirecutters. (SNAP AS PERIMETER FENCE CUT)

Right citizens, stick to the plan. Runway 1, runway 2, nice little lie

down. Fan out, it'll confuse

the fuzz good and proper. One of us will get through.

(AIRCRAFT ROAR AGAIN). Dream liner. Nightmare more

likely. Sweet smell of Kerosene in the morning air. Right, go, go,

go. Move it.

2   **POLICE OFFICER**   Morning, sunshine. Out and about bright and early,

aren't we boys and girls. Spot of fence cutting before breakfast,

stretch your legs on the new runway. All very pleasant I'm sure.

3   **CHAZ**   How did you know we were exactly here?

4   **POLICE OFFICER**   Let's just say a little bird told me.

5   **CHAZ**   You mean…

6   **POLICE OFFICER**   I mean time for an early morning spin to the station

for you lot of smellies. Let's be having you. All aboard the skylark.

(SOUNDS OF SCUFFLES AS PROTESTORS BUNDLED INTO POLICE VAN)

7   **CHAZ**   On what charge?

8   **POLICE OFFICER**   Come along, lad. You don't want to be holding up

all these nice folk on their way to sunny Spain now, do you?

9   **CHAZ**   Freedom of information Act, European Charter of

Human Rights. On what charge are you arresting us, officer?

I demand to know on what charge you are arresting us.

10   **POLICE OFFICER** All these nice *working* people off on their hols to Spain.

(IMITATES CHAZ'S ACCENT) ' I demand to know on what

charge you are arresting us, officer'. Listen you piece of shi…sir.

I, we, everyone has had enough of your rights. Get in the van.

11   **CHAZ**   Section 1 of the charter clearly states…

12   **POLICE OFFICER** Charter flight that would be and you're a common

trespasser**.** In the van now sunshine before I exert my right to ram

the sodding charter up your…

(CACAPHONY OF AIRCRAFT ROAR, POLICE SIRENS
FOLLOWED BY DEAD SILENCE.)

2. INTERIOR. BBC CURRENT AFFAIRS STUDIO. CLASSICAL MUSIC INTRO.
FADE UP DIALOGUE OUT OF MUSIC

1   **CHAZ**   Of course it's all completely different now. Monster supermarkets

making you buy their own plastic bags, I mean we wouldn't want

them in a landfill would we now?

2   **DAME**   Ah, the note of cynicism as the noble lord sinks into the plush red

benches, gliding from law breaker to law maker with effort less

superiority…

Listeners good morning if

you have just tuned in. Today

we have a special treat on air for you. Shining brighter than the sun

through an ozone depleted atmosphere it's Lord Planet saver

himself Lord Charles – Chaz – Hawthorn. Pleasure to have you

with us, Lord Hawthorn.

3	**CHAZ**	Pleasure. Chaz, please.
4	**DAME**	Lord Hawthorn, welcome to '**If I Knew Then What I Know Now**':

the programme where leading public figures look back at the

tipping points in their career, those before and after moments in a

life fully lived when things changed, were never really the same

again, for better or worse.

You are almost single-handedly credited with

moving the whole environmentalism agenda from weirdo fringe

to respectable mainstream. Lord Hawthorn…

5	**CHAZ**	…Chaz…
6	**DAME**	Lord Hawthorn, tell us how the environmental movement is different in 2008 to what, 20, even 30 years ago, apart from the obvious
7	**CHAZ**	The obvious…
8	**DAME**	Suit, hair..
9	**CHAZ**	Well, we all change..
10	**DAME**	..seat in the House of Lords. What was it like to be out there in the beginning?

| 11 | CHAZ | I think it's a very interesting concept. The beginning of a |
| | | movement, any movement. I mean how can any one know at the |

11   CHAZ   I think it's a very interesting concept. The beginning of a

movement, any movement. I mean how can any one know at the

beginning there is even a movement to begin, like punk, raves, like

a happening night club where the hip crowd move on the moment

it becomes hip. At the beginning the movement was so amorphous,

always changing, goals, leaders, leaders arguing there shouldn't be

leaders, those who would put a jacket and tie on, even though were

wearing dreadlocks to go on radio, those who said TV was just a

....

3. GOING BACK IN TIME, CHAZ FIRST TIME ON RADIO,
AN EARLY QUESTION TIME TYPE PROG FROM THE
ARCHIVE

....Yeah, that's just neo-capitalist bollocks. The reality is the

system is contradictory and inherently self destructive. At this

point in history , you, the Establishment, may be under the

impression – a costly mistaken impression – that we are an

unkempt clique of perpetual students who don't join in the

consumerist society because we're not dressed for it. I believe

there will come a time, may be 10, 20, even 30 years from now

when the way I and people like me think and act now will be the

norm. The question is....

12   DAME   The question is...

13   CHAZ   The question is will people, all people, all over the world, choose

to change, to respect the earth, or will it be forced on them at one

minute to midnight as we all drown in a sea of plastic, of shopping

malls, of meaninglessness…

14	**DAME**	Mr, sorry Lord Hawthorn, if I could just bring in Perpetua, who you knew in your street fighting man days all those demos ago. Perpetua….Lord Hawthorn, Charlie to you, of course

15	**PERPETUA**
	SOTTO VOCE	That would be Charlie as in right..

16	**CHAZ**	Perpetua! TO CHAIR It wasn't in the pre –broadcast agreement, in the green room you distinctly said I was the only guest

17	**PERPETUA** That isn't very gentlemanly Charlie, I remember when you were soooooo pleased to see me, and what about that time we were in the power station, blackout and everything and you…

18	**CHAZ**	That was then and this is…really…we must stick to the pre-broadcast agreement…

19	**DAME**	A gentleman's agreement…

20	**PERPETUA** Come now Chaz, you used to be all for transparency, especially when…

21	**CHAZ**	That was then and this is…really I must …CRACKLE AS HE TAKES OUT HIS EARPIECE…

22	**DAME**	And this is now, we'll be right back after this. Don't touch that dial.

CUT TO THEME MUSIC, **CHAZ** CAN BE HEARD STILL REMONSTRATING OFF AIR..

INTRA-RAIL

Templeton shouted the signature on my inter rail pass book, my name as English
–sounding as a vicar calling
'Well hit, sir,'
through a mouth full of honey and tea on the chime of 4.
Apparently.

The feeling I always knew there was something to delayer had led me to divert to this
siding, this square.

It occurs to me how much of my life – time space has been about places, squares, yards,
quads. Place Saint Sulpice, Radhuspladsen, Potsdamer Platz. Standing alone - what's
new – on the outside of this square I reflect on how these places exist objectively.
I'm either in them or looking at them. They exist even if I'm not there to see them, or
anyone else who was there, in these squares, platz, now, in the immediate past, the deep
past, however much of the future is left to me. They'll exist even beyond that, for as long
as they really do exist, whether I'm there or not, to filter, interpret. Sort of psuedy fresher
stuff you might overhear wafting up from the quad, I know, but the traditional inter – rail
rite of passage from student daze to adulthood was far from complete.

I look up from my passbook to the sign at the side of me, the Hoch(high) German gothic
script reminds me of the sign in that bus station in *Where Eagles Dare* (or some other
preposterous *Victor* comic schmaltz, the banal detail of fiction) .

I double-taked:

'Ruprecht Platz

I checked it on the old school book my mother had given me just before I caught the first
train. The style of the handwriting inside the cover, Ilse H, Ruprecht Platz, 1938 was not
a thousand miles away from the style of the signature in my inter-rail book.
It made me smile, I mean, really, 1938 and all that was so long ago smiling must be the
best way to place it this day.

The square a Viennese classic, enclosed, grey concrete walls with windows on 4 sides.
The side I faced was the way in, a proscenium arch, above it the wall - with the entrance
gashed out - and the windows carried on regardless.

I was standing at that point looking in. There wasn't a way out. Particularly if you parked
a 6 wheel military lorry there, crammed with rifles, machine guns, stun grenades and
other bollocks to stop the residents who might just want to saunter out, go to the shops,
post a letter; I mean it was where they lived, the reaction rather extreme, unfair,
unsporting, I thought.

The place seemed designed for the event, that event, some twisto architect looked into the future, drew up a minimalist, brutalist (or is that retro?) block of flats around one entrance to be sealed with one lorry.

' Course it bloody upset me, must have upset millions before me, but I could easily move on with my circular ticket, not like all those other poor souls with their cheap day singles which didn't even entitle them to a seat let alone a compartment like the ones I crashed out in on the overnighters. Yes, alright, I confess put my feet on the seats but no-one saw me.

I was 50% into the Inter-rail month.
London, Aachen, Brussels - decent square that – Cologne, Lyons, Nice, Milan, Innsbruck, Vienna. If this platz really pissed you off that basically piss off back to Nice, overnighter, step out into the Cours Saleya, sun /bikinis /cassis, circle the squares, get a load of that trinity.

Stuck. I could hear it all in my head, a lifetime of tinnitus. The clack of shouldered rifles (no, not ceremonial like that parade square behind St James') the stupid thud of boots, the screams of realisation, women, children, men, young old, cripples, morons – you think I'm going to be PC at a time like this – people being sorted out same as I do with my recycling, tins here, foil there, glass here.

Glass. Crystal clear. I tracked the windows now, hysterically clean, then they must all have been smashed.

Transfixed at that proscenium there was something further, something not quite placed. That was it, grey everywhere. Grey concrete, grey window frames, even the grey chink of permitted sky above.

Suddenly the symmetry of the closed doors was spoiled. One old lady, ashen hair- must be 80s passed through the door carrying a grey bucket – didn't even have a proper watering can for Christ's sake! - . She poured the grey water onto the one artefact of colour in the whole place, a pot of geraniums, the red opening with encouragement.

Time. Time to go move. Back , forward, connection to Nice, emerge into the blue, sky, sea, girls, aperitif time: cassis, a life full of life. My white shirt caught the woman's eye. She moved with surprising deftness,
won our game of stare:

' Guten nachmittag, willkommen zum Platz.' Good Afternoon, welcome to our square.

The sarcasm I learned to survive in the quad came through by reflex –
Can't see what's bloody welcoming about this damn place.

Yet I heard my mouth begin to tell her my name-

Templeton (it must be long after the vicar's tea by now)

'Bitte,'- what-, said the crone.

'Templet….temp….'

She initiated a new game of stare, walk over again. 2 nil. Don't you ever learn? Game over.

'My name is Holzelmacher, I said, dredging up the name that had drifted in from the yard to the kitchen in my childhood semi.

'Bitte, what..?'

'Holzelmacher, my name is…'

Again the deft movement, the hand like a sticky windscreen wiper saying , got it as soon as I saw you.

She repeated my name, rinsed it round her mouth, and after what seemed like 50 years, a smile brought red to her cheeks. She must have been quite a catch in her day.

'Wilkommen', she said, ' wilkommen zum platz.' Welcome..back..to our square.

The geraniums were coming on nicely.

***Intra -Rail** is dedicated to the Hölzelmacher family of Vienna.*

*First developed as **Squaring the Circle**, Skyros, 2008*

Also published in the anthology
__Along the Iron Veins__, www.stairwellbooks.co.uk   York, 2010

Page 4 /4

I-TONE

Late summer, by the pool, a Med resort hotel

A : man 50's

B: woman, late 20s / 30s

The shadows are lengthening in the afternoon sun, only A and B remain on the poolside loungers.

B covered up now, wearing sarong, oversize headphones leak Ibiza style House.

A's dress sense slighty off, OK the linen jacket is Austin Reed but the sleeves up Miami Vice style…

The music from the head phones is audible only as overflow from the headphones – this scene goes on for a long time, B moving along to her own sounds.

Eventually A puts down his Robert Harris novel.

A   Nice. Very handy, very handy device that, very handy.

B   NODDING ALONG , SLIGHTLY TO THE MUSIC

A   WONDERS IF IT IS WORTH TRYING AGAIN

         Handy device that. Very handy. Nice.

B   CONTINUES NODDING AND DRUMMING ALONG TO HER MUSIC

         EVENTUALLY SHE FACES HIM, WITHOUT REMOVING 'PHONES

         Yeah. Right. Very handy.

         RESUMES

         …EVENTUALLY…

A   Loft. Loft, that's where they all end up. In the end.   In the loft.

B   FACES HIM AGAIN, WITHOUT REMOVING PHONES

         Loft?

A   In the end. In the end everything ends up there.

B   What does?

A   Vinyl. LP's, you know, vinyl. You know, just think, imagine, everything in my loft wouldn't

         even fill your device, would hardly trouble it. Imagine.

B   THE MUSIC CONTINUES BUT SHE PAUSES HER MOVES, LOOKS AT HIM, STILL, FOR A LONG

         TIME. THEN RESUMES.

A   Don't mind me. I said don't mind me. No worries, no worries at all.

B   WITHOUT STOPPING What is there to worry about? Mint here, mint.

A   Quite. Mint. Couldn't agree more.

B   HEADPHONES OFF FOR FIRST TIME Sorry you were saying?

A   Nothing.

B   You were saying something.

A   What? Nothing, nothing at all.

B   Just being polite, making conversation, mint place. ' Course if you'd rather not.

A   No, nothing, nothing at all.

B   You were saying something.

         THEY FACE EACH OTHER. EVENTUALLY SHE RESUMES.

A   Handy device that. If you don't mind me saying. Very. Handy.

New Writing original Micro fiction : **I-Tone**

London, 2011

KINDA BLUE

The best title by Miles

12 bars frequented by Mick n' Keef

The waves and beneath until it becomes black

You said I wear it too much

It was how I felt when you left

Read at Spoken Word, York / Radio Ryedale 2006

LID

The way to find what you really need is to leave it all behind.

Almost.

By the sound of a twig beneath a jackboot

-   How do I know that sound when it was my parents who actually heard it-

I calculated I'd about 60 seconds , 90 max.

How did I know this day would come?

I was a child then, the black saucepan you could barely lift was my depository of choice.

Looking back I realise an adult could lift the lid fairly easily

But they thought saucepans were just for soup.

Inside was my manuscript, a brooch from my mother, a watch from my father;

Words, gold, time

-   A heady broth if someone applied fire.

Words, gold, time

These ingredients could heat themselves, fry to a fizz,

Memories too hot to touch, nothing left.

Almost.

LID and PICKED:

Developed at flash fiction workshop, input by Tania Hershman at Jewish Book Week,

London February 2011 and published in

Second Generation Voices

Number 47, May 2011

www.secondgenerationvoices.org.uk

MIKE SPARKS,
POP PROMOTER

Mike Sparks, Pop Promoter is a dramatic monologue in three linked parts

I Baz, II Lady III Sparks

STAGE LIGHTS FLASH IN SILENCE, GRADUALLY WE HEAR TINNY SOUND OF MUSIC THROUGH BAZ ' IPOD, LIGHTS COALESCE TO SPOTLIGHT ON BAZ, HE IS IN WORLD OF HIS OWN, SUDDENLY SEES

AUDIENCE IN FRONT OF HIM, LOOKS OUT , EVENTUALLY TAKES OFF EARPHONES AND SHADES

BAZ-

Sorry couldn't hear you above this, don't want you thinking I've no manners.

STARTS HIS PERFORMANCE

I'm a believer, a believer in letting the music speak but I want to share these unaccompanied words with you all, get my retaliation in first, objectively, before others muddy waters.

You might think this is a bit strange, but then I haven't lived by caring what people think.

The way to remember where we were at is to look at the back of a tee-shirt. At least in my profession, Rock God.

No, listen.

Back of a tee shirt, you know the ones you buy at rock concerts, like Zeppelin London O2,

Stones Madison Square Gardens, Roxy Berlin Rock Palace, that's how I remember where we were.

Diaries? Never my scene, I'm more about Jagger Richards than Blair Campbell or some political dudes.

On the road most nights of the year, absolutely gigging for it. The road.

The scenes just get bigger and bigger. First clubs we played in you could see everyone there – According to the Tee shirt, it says ' my hallway mirror'. No, seriously, you know what I mean. Stadia now , Jesus, Mary and Elvis they're like a town in themselves except they're nowhere. Rotterdam, tee shirts say we were there 3 times, but I've never seen the place, Zurich, Helsinki the same, fly in, check in, sound check, gig, whatever, fly out.

Beijing was different. No, I mean it would be, wouldn't it, if you think about it. I said to the

p romoter three nights, insisted with all the weight of my reputation,

haven't stayed in one place so long since I left school. You have to show respect.

Where it's due.

Give respect to people, give respect to places, I mean , Beijing for Christ's sake, how cool can you get, hip to be square. But that was the mistake. Stopping. In this sharky business you have to keep moving.

I mean moving musically, I mean moving physically. It was the second night when we had the conversation . Or rather we stopped having the conversation.

I can still hear her words now, ringing in my ears like a bad dose of tinnitus –

'I never want to speak to you again', over and over, same doomed chorus, 'I never want to speak to you again.'

'Course I tried to keep it light, merely saying that saying you never want to speak to me again is actually when you think about it speaking to me. That just seemed to really get to her.

Third night she trooped on and sang like a nightingale, but nightingales don't speak either.

The loneliness began to get to me, out there with all the millions of people, the noise, the silence.

By the time I came off after a solo encore on the third night it was scrawled on my dressing room mirror in lipstick. Green lipstick – the only time her taste deserted her.

Capitals screaming back at me 'I never want to speak to you again, I never want to speak to you again,'

The only glimmer of hope was the PS in red , simply one word ' unless...'

That's all I remember about Beijing. It was the last night, that's all I remember.

Haven't heard from her since. I never planned on going solo quite like that.

'Unless...'

I never planned it like that. Never planned anything. Especially going solo. Again.

Let me tell you how it started.

Let me tell you a secret, I always worry about being found out any way.

I'm not a musician, I mean not for real, maybe it was the whole insecure only child thing.

I never paid my dues, served my apprenticeship in the Meccas like Mick and Keith, John and Paul,

Just found I could create an orchestra, a sonic world on my laptop.

TV was my break, not being on it, watching it, I suppose that was the problem later,

I was the original living room legend, notebook and plasma, music on the disk, girls on the walls.

I saw this guy on what was ambitiously listed as a talent show.

Everytime he was on screen a caption came up Mike Sparks , Pop Promoter.

On one of my nights in I saw him interviewed on Sky Arts 2. I'm sure you watch it too.

 He was always addressed as Mike Sparks, not Mike or Sparky – on one show this gorgeous girl called him Mick and he just gave her this look like a laser through rareified air.

 And he always used the same caption,

Mike Sparks, Pop Promoter. The interviewer couldn't handle the word pop and was trying to put words in his mouth like rock, or just to broaden it out a bit, music , even, I think heard this correctly,

art, though it was pretty late by then and I hadn't been out for three days.

Mike Sparks just said, ' it's called popular music for a reason, it's popular, some people have a talent for it. If it's just playing for yourself there's another name for it. I promote pop, some people get rich by doing it properly, me included. Problem?'

When I talked to my friend he said yeah, millions of people hate Mike Sparks, he's so popular.

I downloaded my album, put it in an envelope to the channel, addressed Mike Sparks , Pop

Promoter.

17 nights later I had an email with attachment heading ' how big do you really wannabe – open this and change your world ' - I don't normally open emails like that but I did and it did.

It simply read 'the way you can make money is finding your soul. I'll introduce you to her.'

There was a picture of a gorgeous girl, did I know her, not from real life but from somewhere parallel? Podcast, Facebook, YouTube , TV? - I wasn't totally sure, I have it on day and night but rarely watch it.

The attachment looked like some contract, I kind of remember the zeros, I don't really do words.

Mike Sparks choppered me into Shepperton and said, 'Baz, this is Lady, just remember she's called Lady for a reason.' I was never in the same room as him again.

 It was the wisest thing anyone has ever said to me.

We had one rehearsal, her vocals soared above the beats like a dream. I never woke up...in time.

The first proper name of all time on the tee shirt was Leeds Academy. I t was just a bigger room, with Lady in it, and I learned the job on the job, learned to love the world and it reciprocated.

Until...until Beijing.

Looking back I should have seen it coming. Maybe I should never have moved in above the shop;

 the tee shirts don't speak the full story, touring is a bubble of loneliness.

Yeah, you heard me first take, touring is lonely in that surrounded by millions never alone drugs don't work type loneliness, especially in Beijing.

At least it has been since the lipstick. The green and the red on that theatre style make up mirror the one with the bulbs round it like a garland of bright ideas except this one wasn't, not the way I saw it. 'Unless...'

 I never planned it. There are ways of going solo, different types of being solo, I've tried most, duos are best.

'There's a reason why Lady is called Lady.'

It really freaks me out, did then, still does, people - intimate strangers – tweet talking me and saying you had it all: sex – no not sex, love , money, musical recognition, whatever you wanted – and , they say, you deliberately blew it. That's what these fans, these strangers say. Blew it, like driving a Rolls into a pool but infinitely more significant. Let me tell you about me and Lady, I'm tired of you hearing it from others. Not everyone has my best interests a t heart. Lady did. Always.

I realise that now she's gone.

Lady and I had been together ever since the beginning. Lady was the beginning, like Eve, only better dressed.

I admit we weren't to be pantheoned with the all time greats musically, Mick and Keith, John and Paul, Elton and Bernie, Baz and Lady , no , I do most shit but not blasphemy. I wrote the songs, taught the band from the keyboard. We didn't make it big, we were big from day one. When Lady floated in on vocals the magic started. Magic came into the band, into my life, the journey started, the road came up to meet us. I moved in on lady and she moved in. On the road, on stage, hotels with more stars than any galaxy but still hotels. I wrote the music for our first number one-

'I said I'd love you forever, you said it wasn't long enough.'

Retrospectively there may have been an ambivalence in Lady's lyric, interpretations aren't static, you learn that as you go along.

Yeah, I did look at other women – sometimes twice – I'm not a fool, but looking isn't buying.

If we 'd simply done the usual one nighter in Beijing we'd still be on the road now. Coming off stage it's usually a beer, okey dokey maybe a little something a bit stronger since your're twisting my arm.

And that – I swear - is all it was, exit stage left and my arm around Mike Smart's Head of Asia Pacific, third night, I mean we were rocking Beijing for Christ's sake, if it wasn't for Xing it wouldn't have happened, that's what I said to Lady.

She said if it wasn't for her I'd be Mr Nowhere and disappeared into the square – heavenly I think they call it in translation. I was lost for words.

Next morning about 4 in the afternoon I saw it in Paris Match, the only photo of the whole event, me and Xing entwined, like I'd done it all myself.

I hadn't woken up alone since Lady and I first went to bed together. It was so cold I broke out into a sweat. I filled up her voicemail but you just know when people are never going to return your calls.

I drank my way back to London, still the ringing silence.

There's no business like show business, we – the remnants - were due onstage in 15 minutes – let's see, yeah, Vienna, - means nothing to me - looked like an evening of instrumentals with no lady on vocals when she rang.

'I'm just ringing to tell you I never want to speak to you again'

But you are I said, sort of jerk thing you say when you are so relieved. ' Get your sweet arse out here, we're on in 15'

'That all you care about, Baz, what about the past, what about the future?'

'Lady, what's got into you? We live and love for the moment, we always have, you know us'

'Comes a time, Baz' she said, voice a way I'd never heard before, flat, off key.

'Sing Babe, we'll talk minute we get off stage.'

'Like we did in Beijing?'

' I admit I put my arm round the promoter's assistant, come on Babe, coming off stage, biggest gig since..'

'That how you see me, *Babe, your* assistant? '

'What has got into you, Lady? We're on in 5, we've never missed a show.'

'First time for everything'

'What can I say to make it all right, make it like it was before?'

'It isn't like it was before. What can you do, Mr Solo man? You can see how it feels, the Beatles were wrong'

'Babe, Lady?'

''All you need is love' - come to think of it they got it right too – ' give me money, that's what I want'- how much is the difference between a dinosaur and a god..?'

'I wrote the music, without music there's nothing.'

' You can't write magic and I don't like finding out what's in Swiss bank accounts in one name. Actually two names and mine isn't one of them.

You just keep me hanging on. Maybe that's life, at least it's your life, started solo, end up solo, bastard Baz, see what it's really like with no Lady in your life, in 5, 4 minutes.., unless...'

'Unless?'

'If you have to ask, I'm not going to say this twice, I never want to speak to you again.'

There was no encore that night. No amp could fill the big silence, all the instruments sounded flat.

The thrill had gone.

-Mike Sparks Pop \promoter I page 7/7

II LADY

I remember how we started, hot summer night, singing the blues, room above a room in a pub.

Riverside, Putney Bridge, decentish crowd – I mean the size, not their manners – some new faces, I like that, keeps it flowing, I've always preferred rivers to lakes.

I want to get to it – I know Baz is out there somewhere gigging to tell you his side of the song-

Must be some hope for us, first time I haven't used the word Bastard in front of his name for a while-

alliterative vocalists habit, Bastard Baz, he's not a bad man, he' s just ambitious, o r maybe that's a more accurate description of Mick Sparks but , hey, let's get the lyric out before I default into all men are bastards riff, too many sisters cruising on that.

Yeah, Putney Bridge, doesn't alliterate off the vocal like Stockholm Superdrome or Bakersfield Bowl but size isn't everything. In fact I liked the beginning much more than the end, the venues, the crowd, the chance of hope, everything in front of you. When it happens, that moment when everything is going to change for the bigger you have to step up, you 'll corpse if you swan around in the lake for too long. If it doesn't happen you can stay, lucky you not having to make a choice yourself, if it does you have to go whatever the consequences.

First up: I assure you I'm objective but you may find this incredible – at that time I had no idea who Mike Sparks was. I t was a Tuesday night, I'd had what the landlord called a residency in the Riverside Pub for a while. I auditioned for it but the landlord rather gallantly told me after there was no contest, Tuesday night the most difficult to fill a pub so bleakly equidistant for weekends past and to come.

By no contest, he recovered, he meant he'd heard a spark in my phrasing – rumour was he resided at Ronnie Scotts some sixties Tuesday and knew all about phrasing: when it rises, peaks, falls, rises again...

It's yours he said. When can you start?

-How about Tues...well, you know, I said and my weeks were never the same again.

Atmospheres are really something for a singer, you can reach out and touch them, do you make them or they make you?

On my night I learned how to cook up a storm, other nights fell flat but you learned on the job.

I kind of prided myself on that, I don't mean this to sound off but I thought Billie and Ella must have come through Speakeasys like that. I was going to say not like kids nowadays who seem to come from nowhere but I made a deal with myself not to become the sort of artist who says ' nowadays '.

That Tuesday there was something in the air. I was only doing my job but the landlord did say word was out and regulars were beginning to complain how difficult it was to get through the weekend with Tuesday so remote.

We were deep into ' 'Cry me a River '' when the bassist gushed ' Mike Sparks is in the house', the neck of the Fender craning towards this cat in a Paul Smith shirt stage left.

Between numbers I almost fired him, I said there must be a least, well I don't know how many folks in the house and we play to one and all not one. (Truth be told I never felt the bassist was one of the brotherhood – there was that Tuesday when he said he couldn't make it and offered to rig up a sampler to fill in. I said where else is so important for you on a Tuesday night).

First thing Mike Sparks ever said to me was –

-I can't come back after the interval and you can't go on, there isn't going to be a second half. Not here, well, maybe some instrumentals. For them – he swept his arm across the pub floor, the strobe picked out two or four faces, happy Tuesdays

-They're my people , I replied, I owe them...

-	They owe you, i f they're your people they'll multiply and follow you. Trust me.

I don't feel why but I did. Mike Sparks was like that, birds out of the trees to mint a phrase.

He held this printout in front of me, with each flash of the strobe there seemed to be another nought on the end of a sentence or was that just my imagination..

-	I'll give you everything you want. Except time. For now. You can buy that later. Trust me.
	Sign here, I'll have a car for you in the morning, we'll cross the River Sticks'

Yeah I know, people who say 'Trust me ' are like people who say 'Respect'. Everything about him screamed ' don't' and it wasn't just the shirt.

O f course I signed in a flash. Tuesdays were never the same again.

And of course there wasn't a car waiting for me next morning – it was the only time Mike Sparks actually lied to me, yeah there were omissions, cutbacks on the verite, but no lies. No car- the chopper landed by the river- and , of course no Mike Sparks, he was already on the tarmac at Shepperton.

Next to him was this guy with white skin – as the shadow of the slowing rotors washed over him he seemed like a telly on the blink.

Mike Sparks set it up.

'Lady, this is Baz, Baz this is Lady. Always remember she's called Lady for a reason. The gear is ready in sound stage one. I'll let you out when you're ready.'

I 'll be straight with you, I didn't take to Baz immediately, maybe it was just the impression he was more used to machines than women, I'd com e up through playing in bars. He'd obviously impressed everyone in his bedroom but I surmised Mike Sparks must have figured he wouldn't get a return on his investment unless Baz demechanised.

We worked on a few sounds – I wouldn't call them tunes at that point – with me on vocals like that lyric –less way Pink Floyd used way back. It worked for them.

I could hear we had potential, once Baz even looked up from some machine and made eye contact,

Some kind of magic? Possibly.

'We need words , ' was all he said. I hadn't expected it from him. I looked at him for a while. He held my look. ' Words, he said, ' it isn't what I do.'

'I need a break,' I said, sound stage one was like hangar, it didn't seem to bother Baz that much

I tried the door marked Exit, when it opened it didn't let in any light. In the frame was a man so huge he blocked out the sun. He spoke –

'Mr Sparks thought you might want these.' In one hand was a bottle of Evian, the other a notebook with pen. I made to walk past him, it was beginning to seem like a long time since I'd seen the sun.

What is it with these sunless guys?

'Mr Sparks looks forward to your product, have a nice day.'

The door closed, I had no way of knowing if it was day or night. Sometimes things are decided for you, you just have to go with them, you can only choose to do it with or without grace.

I replayed Mike Spark's voice-

''Remember she's called Lady for a reason.''

I don't know if the sun went down that night or not but Baz seemed to hit a groove and I saw my hand move across the page –

''You said you'd love me forever

I said that's not long enough.''

I didn't love Baz at first, but it came like it might eventually in a successful arranged marriage if you stick at it beyond what it was arranged for.

One night, Jesus, Mary and Elvis -where were we? – I looked across the stage, all I remember that made that one different to the ones before was it was open air, San Francisco, San Antonio, San whatever- Baz working the keyboards, his face like I'd never seen it before, brown.

Don't let people tell you everything is about money. It's all about time. At least in the beginning, but in the beginning is the – my – end. When couples become inseparable is when things can fall apart.

When I suggested moving in with him, Baz remarked, well, Mike Sparks will like it, halving the hotel overheads and smiled. I said leave the humour to me Baz, humour is words, he said he wasn't being funny.

Halcyon days, touring the world, we never missed a beat, the road rising up to meet us en route to Beijing. Of course you can only see the end of the road with hindsight, on the road it's just one night after another. But Beijing was different – you 'd expect it to be.

Maybe stuff had being going wrong before then, too wide eyed to see it coming, I'd been promoted to too big a stage too quickly, maybe...but when we came off that first night and I saw Baz with his arm round Xing I flipped. Big time. I'd done the passive – my aggressive is to disappear, thinking it will hurt whoever I 'm angry with but 'course that turns out to be me.

Don't ask me about the Swiss bank account thing, it has Mike Sparks written all over it but maybe

Baz wasn't such a child after all. Baz used to give me a wage like an old fashioned house wife got her dosh on a Friday night. I just accepted it. Baz does the music, I do the lyrics, must have been Mike Sparks who did the maths – I wouldn't put anything beyond him. He's tone deaf.

Back in London I threw my mobile in the Thames you know the way they do in the movies.

There isn't much point in screaming '' I never want to speak to you again'' then checking your voicemail every 7 minutes. I regretted it later, wished I'd bribed a scuba diver to bring it up, Baz wasn't a bad man, we were a good duo, trios always end badly.

I found the flyer saying ' Baz live in Soho' washed up on the river bank. I'd stopped singing by then – don't know why I went but I'd nothing to do that Tuesday. Did I want something? Money, Justice, a return to the beginning?

The club was as sunless as that hangar in Shepperton, I could feel there wasn't a ray of hope...

Unless...unless Baz offered to make it right, I believed it was in his power, in his nature, maybe it wasn't by then, too much water under the bridge.

You start solo, you end solo, if there is a duet in the middle you'r e a lucky star.

The only light came from one spot, Baz uplugged, singing almost to himself, the sight, the sound, the lyric gave me no pleasure, I hadn't realised how finite it was –

''I said I'd love you till the end of time

You said it wasn't long enough.''

LADY

Part 2 of the 3 part monologue Mike Sparks, Pop Promoter. Page 5/5

Acknowledgement :ADL, 2011

III SPARKS

IN HIS LONDON OFFICE, NIGHT- WE CAN READ THE BACK TO FRONT
LETTERING '' MIKE SPARKS, POP PROMOTER, WARDOUR STREET, LONDON'' -
THROUGH LIGHT SHINING THROUGH THE GLASS ON THE DOOR –GLINT OF
GOLD DISCS ON THE WALL AND EMPTY CHAMPAGNE BOTTLE

ON THE PHONE FEET UP ON DESK BACK TO AUDIENCE ONLY LIT BY DESK
LAMP

'What time is it there Baz, don't you sleep anymore? Trust me, in my experience people who
repeatedly say '' I never want to speak to you again '' mean '' speak to me, tell me sweet
things, tell me something new '', what they really really don't mean is ''I never want to speak
to you again''. Leave it with me, Baz. No Baz that isn't a good idea, you've just come off
stage, you're as high as the sky, biggest gig since...yeah...whatever it says on the tee-
shirt...yeah, man...listen...that's a mistake Baz, I think you'll find you do need ...especially
now... I know, trust me...Baz...Baz...?'

PHONE DOWN, HE TWISTS LAMP INTO MICROPHONE SHAPE AND CROONS

' ' You said you'd love me till the end of time, I said I'd paid you too much''

WHILE MOCK PLAYING(pc) KEYBOARD ON HIS DESK.

 SILENCE, HE ATTEMPTS TO POUR A GLASS OF CHAMPAGNE FROM THE EMPTY
BOTTLE.

LIGHTS DOWN, SPARKS HEAD ON DESK ASLEEP.

THREE SPOT LIGHTS UP TO FULL, ONE ON SPARKS. SPARKS STARTS AS IF
SUDDENLY AWARE SOMEONE IN ROOM

Lady? That you?

SILENCE. LIGHTS DOWN. SLEEPS ON DESK AGAIN. PHONE RINGS, HE LEAVES
IT.

ONE LIGHT GRADUALLY UP ON SPARKS. SPARKS SWIVELS ROUND IN EAMES
CHAIR AND STARES STRAIGHT OUT AT AUDIENCE WITH LASER STARE.

NOW COMPOSED   HE 'BREAKS' THE SILENCE AND ADDRESSES AUDIENCE
FOR FIRST TIME

Do forgive me, you must think me terribly crass, please allow me to introduce myself, I'm a
man of wealth *and* taste. Mike Sparks, Pop Promoter. You heard that first take. Pop . Not
House Music of Black Origin Urban Garage Grind never mind the bollocks wham: – pop.

It's popular, – and the 'artistes' make a shed load, you lot have a dance, no worries, everyone happy.

Wealth *and* taste, which one wouldn't you believe – look here's the keys to my Roller, the yellow one outside, can't miss it, registration MS POP1, have a joyride, bring it back, I trust you. Trust me.

Lady ? You want to talk about Lady? Suits me. Make yourself comfortable, Uncle Mike will tell you

all about it. Yeah, all. The beginning? First thing you need to understand is Baz and Lady were a

Trio. The third man? Yours truly, Mike Sparks, Pop Promoter. I'm as creative as the other two – and not just with the accounts. Without me it would never have happened, trust me. I mean never have happened at all, not just a bit on a different scale, down the bill on the northern club circuit, I mean not at all. Lady? Yeah a real Lady I grant you, a real Lady with perfect pitch – yeah, so? Baz, a hero in his own bedroom, genius, yeah, so? Remember the old vinyl LPs? : 33 1/3, 33 1/3, 33 1/3, there is a reason, holy trinity , one third each. I found them both, introduced them, lit the touch paper and retired , mainly to the south of France. Without me, nothing. A trio, we could have called it the Mike Sparks Experience but that's been done before and the only thing that used to keep me awake at night was vulgarity.

There is no recipe for magic.

I don't sing, I don't play an instrument – who does nowadays – I don't dance - give thanks –

It's the opposite of a problem. Djs are stars, all that Ibiza lark - in these terms they don't do anything either.

I'm as much a part of the trio as the other two, in the beginning was The Spark. Without getting into some kinda radio three late night zone, we live in a post –textual world: managing the talent is the same as having it. This is getting to sound defensive. Let's get back to the sequence.

Lady was Lady before I invented the name. Lady is always *the* Lady. I've always admired good manners. And yes you can believe what you read in the papers – I took out the advert in the posh Sundays ' There is no truth in the rumour of the relationship between myself yours truly Mike Sparks, and Lady.' And that isn't just Clintonesque read my lips semantics. Trust Me. I bought Lady in to Baz as an artiste; magic can't be explained, I create environments where it can happen.

PHONE RINGS INSISTENTLY, FOR AN INSTANT SPARKS MOVES TO ANSWER IT, THEN LEAVES IT UNTIL IT STOPS RINGING.* (RING TONE SONG)

Where were we, where were they? Yes, Beijing, first night.

I made it happen, I made them take the step up. Without me…What? Come on, a Swiss bank account is just a means to an end, everyone has one, don't they? I took it out in my name and Baz' to make him grow up. Quick. How Baz and Lady in the group arrange their finances is their affair. I thought we'd moved on from this, I don't need the hassle.

It wasn't like you might think, it all happened so quickly, we made the plans after everything happened. Post hoc. The magic of Lady's voice and poise, the rythmn and textures of Baz' soundscape.

Mix, stir, simmer, wow! You can't analyze that.

Since you ask I never had a problem with Lady moving in with Baz, not ideal professionally speaking,

But no need for me on the road these days anyway.

I never knew an act get so big so quickly. I just stayed in London – I had a map on the table of where they were , like those old wartime ops room with WAAFs and WRENS moving the shapes around to indicate where they were with a red phone for Baz and a black phone for Lady.

It was the Chinese ambassador who came to me, I told you people always come to me in the

end; come to me in the beginning and in the end, I don't do middles.

Beijing was a triumph, it's a bit of a blur now, biggest thing I ever did – and best – delegation to an assistant isn't exactly my style but I was getting less sleep than Live Aid era Geldof, gave the details to Xing, thought she did a good job, they all did.

You never know you're at a turning point at the time, whatever it is , music, business, life, hindsight doesn't exist, life is just a sequence of nows, but things were never the same after Beijing.

I've never gone public about this before – unprofessional disclosure – but since I'm among friends exactly one year A B , After Beijing - the truth can now be told. Baz phoned me, I don't know what time of the day or night it was or what he was on at that time, he just said, I don't need you anymore, I'm a musician, you know what, I don't need anyone.

I told him to get some rest, get with Lady, get home.

I don't like people telling me they don't need me when they so obviously do, it isn't a smart move to do that to Mike Sparks, trust me, it's better I tell you in advance rather than you find out yourself too late.

I'll always have time for Lady. Still.

INSISTENT PHONE RING AGAIN. SPARKS 'STARES' IT OUT.

Now? Baz? No, I don't owe him anything, and it was him who said he didn't need me.

Lady? Yeah, I spoke to her on the phone recently.

Someone new? Maybe. Time waits for no one, you gotta move, keep moving to be a player in this game.

Yeah, Lady and I, lunch at the Wolseley, said Baz trying to get the bread together for a suitable venue for a comeback gig. I listened but of course I already knew. I know everything. Trust me.

Comebacks are for has beens who shouldn't have.   That's the past. I don't go there. Hindsight? What's the use? Yesterday's gone.

I knew Baz was dying out there, little club just round the corner from here - Wardour Street.

 Could it have been any different? I told you , he said he didn't need me.

Sometimes corpsing is the only way to stay alive. One day they'll both thank me, they just can't see it yet. Trust me.

SPOTLIGHTS DOWN , ONLY NEON LIGHT S OUTSID E

*Part III of **Mike Sparks , Pop Promoter,** page 4 / 4*

Thanks to ADL, AR, Arvon, Script Factor York.

Also available online at-

bushgreen.org

and

ABCTales.com

Mike Sparks Pop Promoter/ I II III.

Other work with a musical theme includes -

As If (Riff I), Soft Machine (*in* **Wise Guy and other fables)**

And

High C *(in* **Platform Free)**

OFF THE BUSES

If pushed I'd say it was when you started your new year fitness regime it all began to go wrong.

Leaping off the bus three stops earlier than usual, you seemed so resolute.

You responded to my

'I'll love you till the end of time'

With

'That's not long enough' , hedging with finites.

As the bus drew away you said it feels nearer the end than the beginning.

I said 'Stop this right now; do you know what you are doing..?'

Eventually you reduced the number of stops so much you weren't getting on the bus at all.

After you'd gone I realised I couldn't hope to keep up

The only thing I hate is 'ifs'

PICKED

I'm just a kid like any other

Asking my Mum questions, looking for answers

That's how you learn, that's what I was told.

Where's Alfons now, I asked next morning before it got too hot to stay inside-

It felt a bit annoying to be cheated out of an uncle.

Why did he get on the wrong train-

He's just a kind like any other – was he all alone,

Weren't there any other nice people to help him?

Mum said not everyone was nice then in this city where she came from;

Situations can happen where some bad people do bad things.

Situations?

He was just a kid like any other.

Did someone pick on him?

Didn't anyone stand up for him?

Where did his train end up?

Why..?

Not every question has answers my Mum said.

I went outside to set up the wickets.

It was the longest day; that night the stars didn't bother.

Upstairs

I practiced his name out loud for when I could meet him:

Alfons

In time with the Strauss from the Schiedmayer below

Me and Alfons,

We're just kids like any other.

I couldn't sleep for the light.

For Alfons Holzelmacher

Born Vienna 8.11.1930

Died Auschwitz 1944

SHAFT 247

REPORTER   ...the wheel of fortune that dealt the miners this turn of fate is turning in their favour, each revolution of the wheel spinning from darkness to light, the wheel of life that...

REP IN HAND TO EARPIECE GESTURE AS NEWS CONTROL ROOM FEEDS IN

CONTROL ROOM   Cut this tombola bollocks, if I have to mention this again you're off the story. It's not circles we want it's angles, human angles, that means S E X , slag heaps of it if possible, mine the seam , give me riches, pan to gold...

REP   (FILLING) ...Emilio Estevez, Sancho Panchez, Diego Riviera...

CONTROL   Yeah, sounds like the one, is he out yet?

REP   (STILL FILLING).. the wheel of honour Santiago De Compostella, Pantella de...ASIDE TO CONTROL A shaft full of blokes in darkness only experienced by other blokes like submariners or students on Countdown sofa –curtains drawn in the afternoon- marathons: You sure there is a sex angle buried in this one, boss? Must be your subconscious...(RESUMES FILLER ON AIR) Sigmundo Neros...

CONTROL   OK, 30 second ad break- Don't you read the blogs? Guy down there with wife and mistress who just met on the surface, waiting for him to emerge, it doesn't get any better than that, for us that is. I'll feed you, 3,2, live-

REP   I counted them all out, only , what 5 to go , make that 4, latest phoenix just risen, light at the end of the tu...

CONTROL   His name is Angelo – I am not making this up, wife Maria, Mistress Bianca, Jesus, I'm paying you on location, give me the story...

REP   Make that 3, make that 2, last man rising is Angelo Amores, rumour has it not only is his wife waiting for him here at Camp Surface but his mistress too, Camp Furnace, yes, it's confirmed all the miners accounted for and the last man Angelo Amores is about to commence the journey from the underworld to...the wheel is turning, I've never seen the wheel turn that fast, must be so light, wait, the cage has opened, just a note, it's been translated now, yes, ..'Thank you dear rescuers but I'm staying here.' Unbelievable scenes here , underground since the summer, sunstarved , but volunteering to remain in the dark. Wait...another message, they're pleading with him to come up; ...'it is only in the darkness I can see the light...'...'the sun is my mind, lit by searing memories...'...'only in darkness is beauty eternal'...Angelo Amores is not, repeat not coming to the surface, the rescue is not complete, there is one man still to come, the authorities...two women...choosing hell rather than heaven...

CONTROL   Nice, liking it, follow the story, deeper. Go. Do it, Go..or I'll ...where the sun never shines...

REP TO CONTROL ...No, boss, down into that hell? No..., what an angle.. SIGNAL
FAINT, Hell.. DESCENT

SHORE THING

The sea is always the sea, grey or blue

The sky is always the sky, blue or grey

You are you, constantly

Each wave is unique, it will never happen again

Though I am glad I saw that one , and that one and...

Time ticks on, but if you just count one wave after another you wouldn't think so

And what about that moment when the wave stops crashing forward but hasn't slunk back?

Still.

I first came here so many years ago

I went away but never left

You wave hello, you wave goodbye, just floating along

It isn't the sea that's dangerous, it's the coast.

Is it the sky that colours the sea

Or the other way round?

Things can be said without a sound

Grey become blue

 Beached, between waves, a dash to collect pebbles

Look! That one is shaped like a heart

I put it back, I know you'll say it was just a stone

That one is like a ...that one like a ...

Soon I had so many, heavy with shapes

Should I put them back where they belong? Exactly.

 Before someone notices they have gone?

-Said you rearranged the beach!

Quickly

This moment before the next wave erases everything

Shore Thing (& Wave Back Then & Good bye Wave) is part of The Wave sequence,

Nice 2010..

SUNNY GOOD FRIDAY

Some roads are lined with Hibiscus

Others with thorns

Some you can read on the map

And you make all the right connections-

It really is no trouble at all.

Some roads are long

Some hard

Some wide

The difference may not be as important as you imagine

The unfamiliar road as difficult

As the one you knew well

Canary islands, Easter 1996

ISBN 0 7951 5227 2

THE GREATEST HIT:
FEATURING **JUNIOR WADE**

Wade was in The Zone. He loved music, Wade *is* music. He loved music, the guys in band, loved Gloria. That's inverse order. Gloria wasn't another woman, she was *the* woman, the one who all the songs were about. Wade loved her more than he liked, more than he knew right now but there's no future in fighting facts.

Doesn't matter how many times you go out there in any gig there is always The Zone.

When that's gone you stop.

The band opened with the traditional homage ' Crossroads', blasted through ' Gloria On My Mind' - wonder what that's all about – and were grooving into the second lick of 'Honey and Jet' when the bass player invaded Wade's spot.

'You're in my face, man' said Wade through the monitor back channel. It's true that music biz chestnut about how Junior Wade sacked a bass player mid riff and the keyboard player was paid double that night for improvising on the deep reverb pedal. You never stand in Wade's spot. Never. Don't go there.

There is always a first time.

'We need to get you off stage , man' said the bass player, 'platform gantry gonna go.'

Wade glared back 'You're in my face, bro.'

'Close the riff, man, now, off stage left, close the riff, that way there'll be no panic.'

Wade never missed a beat.

Glastonbury was the big one. It's not a gig, it's pinnacle city, next stop heaven. Yeah some cat onstage droned through the emergency procedures but who listens to that? Ever listened to the flight attendants tell you where the oxygen is, who has that kinda time?

The gantry was in Junior's face before the riff was out. That line about ' you see your life flash before you just before you die, gig over, next stop Big Man in the sky ' – there can only be one way to check it out. It's the same point about accidents: are you lucky because the gantry missed your neck main arterial or a jerk because the gantry crashed on you and not some hanger –on 4th rate bongo player in the first place?

There is something about the unified silence of a huge crowd, the stillness of terror.

Wade was on the deck in less than a second, the left side of his face slashed to the neck. He was down and out. Thank Christ the paramedics were smoother movers than that 60s dinosaur support band. Blood staunched or at least controlled the stretcher was on.

'Sir, we need to move you now,' said the lead para.

You got to give it up for Junior. He couldn't stand up but he'd grown up. His pre-surname appellation suddenly seemed so unfair.

'Damn right boy we need to move, gimme the mic..'

'Sir, I don't advise…'

'Gimme the mic, God damn…'

Wade had spent his whole life – up to now – getting what he asked for , even if this was his last request it wasn't going to be any different. You don't mess with the big man even when he might be about to meet the Biggest Man of all the other side of an intensive care unit.

He could hardly move, flat out on the stage like a horizontal martyr fallen from the top of the London Eye, but praise the Lord the wound seemed shut at last. Some neck.

'Listen up, folks', that charm of Junior's North London going on Southern Louisiana drawl was unaffected. The crowd turned with one face. 'Listen up, folks. I don't know if it's my time, I ain't afraid to meet the good Lord time of his choosing, but if it is or if it ain't I .. I .. gotta say one word to y'all..'

Wade was woozy, black in a pool of red. It was painful to see him grounded. Would he go before the one word was transmitted? 'Folks, I wanna tell ya..one word..Gloria. You gotta love your woman, above all, worship her, stay close..' The image swam into him, the raven hair, the swan-like movements, the dewdrop sweat (couldn't the woman stop being elegant for once!) – on the black brows as she gave him young Marty, their first born, the beauty, the honour of her black triangle. The image pulled Wade forward to the microphone for one more surge. ' You gotta, let me tell you people, you gotta..Gloria, glori', sister morphine beginning her sweet riff, rippling through Junior Wade, the ultimate music.. 'Gloria..glori..'

Developed at Skyros 2008 and read at Aesthetica Speakers' Corner, York March 2009.

UP MEMORY LANE

The spiral staircase was such a downer. Lane trekked up – 14, 15, 16, 18, 19, 20 ..same as his age.

At the top he had to shoulder the stuck door open. The room made his heart skip a beat before it sank. Oxford, city of lost causes, the college a 14th century foundation, always had the adjective 'prestigous' dumped in front of it. Lane had no time for prestige, a concept, a waste of time; prestige is something that doesn't work properly.

…23, 24…'the journey of a thousand miles begins with a single step.'

He dragged himself into the gloom of his room. The bed was single, a monk bed it shouted at him, lost cause, double is a waste of space, like Lane himself, his thoughts spiralling out of control regardless of any assertive techniques they'd filled him up with at the crammer.

Lane drew back the curtains, the reflex of moving into a Marriot or Best Western or some other beige. He had to smile: behind the curtains was a picture, a view of the college, not bad actually, a water colour signed by some fellow, depicting the quad in May, a scene of open panes and window boxes.

'Yeah, hard Brie and all that, bloody door's a bastard too. Still, expect you'll hardly be in here, ' said the incoming tall figure, flashing a smile, not a wink , at the bed.

Lane turned. The figure seemed to have glided in, the door no issue for him.

'Terence Honeyman-Scott..', the hand beyond the cufflinks surprisingly firm.

'Lane.'

'..zillion syllables I know,' said Honeyman – Scott, ' let's just leave it as Tez. I'm across the hall, almost room mates, calls for a snifter before dinner. Join us, drinks, dinner, post-prandial cruise over to Charlie's for an Armagnac or 4?'

The inflection of Honeyman-Scott's requests were statement like.

Lane followed 'Tez' across the landing. Immediately in his room he drank in the view.

Oriel window wide open, dappled evening light, fragrance from the flowers on the sills beyond it, the distinctive chime of the cathedral bells in the near distance.

Tez hovered over his Vermouth long enough to register Lane's reaction to the view, the discrepancy between the two rooms.

Tez mimed a perfect forward defensive cricket stroke. 'You haven't got to take these issues personally, Lane. It's just the way things are.'

Lane's reflection on how immediately he was an unhandled surname and Honeyman-Scott a self allocated catchy nickname was interrupted by the on hour chimes of the bells.

Dinner seemed to slide down Tez's silk scarfed throat.

Lane walked, Tez glided along the High to Charlie's college.

It was Charlie who shook hands with Lane, her hands so fabulous that silk gloves would just make them feel rough. It may have been the second Vermouth but Lane felt sure the handshake went on a millisecond longer than necessary.

'Charlotte, everyone calls me Charlie. So you're Tez's room mate.'

'Well, across the hall actually but..'

'Mmm how divine, wish this college had gone co-ed, mind you a landing between Tez and I would just be a waste of space.'

Lane never felt three to be a crowd though he did recall turning down the fifth Armagnac.

Lane came down with a borderline 2:1, ie a 2:2. The alumni web chronicled Charlie and Tez for a couple of years – a cricket blue for him, a first for her, then they disappeared off the radar. Lane – if and when he thought of it at all - had this image of them moored in a clipper off a Caribbean island but they weren't the waters Lane sailed in and radar wasn't designed for silhouettes like that. He worked, tubed, bed-sitted and didn't take it personally; it's just the way things are. His acronymed institute wasn't the smartest of places. In his office his door blown by a Mistral type draught clanked against a filing cabinet. Lane's econometrics wasn't exactly Nobel prize calibre but refereed journals here, invitations to address New Labour there at least earned him a top floor office. If you stood on a stash of New Statesman's and craned out of the attic style window you could almost see Big Ben.

The office opposite , from where you actually could see Big Ben was currently being refurbished for a Spring arrival, pretty hot stuff it was rumoured, double barrel, Honey –something. It was on the stroke of May when the director of the Institute pushed open Lane's door and introduced his new colleague. He seemed out of breath, perhaps because the lift was out of order..

'Charlotte Honeyman – Scott, Lane, Lane, Charlotte. She'll be just across the landing from you.'

Charlie reached out her hand, Lane held her eyes.

'It's just the way things are,' she smiled.

It was all a long time ago - now.

Developed from a workshop on Skyros 2008, > Oxford / London2011

WATER UNDER THE BRIDGE

When the Spring came

The river unmuddied itself

I could see the bicycle beneath the surface

I pictured the day when the owner must have wheeled it proudly home

The first time

Perhaps a gift

Of movement, poise, balance, purpose.

What must have flowed since

To bring it to its fathomed end?

River Ouse, Spring 2011

WAVE BACK THEN

If you see the wave coming in to shore
There is a point
When it is still-
Silent-
Then moves back
Starts all over again
Same wave but different.

A still point
Silence, golden sand
An eternity
At the edge of the sea, the edge of the land.

If you look in a mirror
There is a flicker
When your eyes move
From surface to self.
A still point
But can you hold your own gaze
After all these years?

Be still, be silent
An eternity
When there is positively no reflection
No sound, no movement
 No words, no wave
Nothing doing, anything going, nothing
 To regret.

Whitby, (after Paul Nash painting Winter Sea, York Art Gallery) 2010

MICRO-WAVES

J F T King

I would like to thank everyone who has helped me along the way.

York European Publishing

ISBN 978-0-9558519-3-3

End photo:

The author at Skyros Writers' Lab, 2008

© 2012

www.ingramcontent.com/pod-product-compliance
Lightning Source LLC
Chambersburg PA
CBHW041011070726
47599CB00025BA/50